I dedicate this book to my mother, Lana Irene.
Thank you, Mom.

Balboa Press books may be ordered through booksellers or by contacting:

Balboa Press
A Division of Hay House
1663 Liberty Drive
Bloomington, IN 47403
www.balboapress.com
844-682-1282

ISBN: 979-8-7652-3474-7 (sc)
ISBN: 979-8-7652-3475-4 (e)

Print information available on the last page.

Balboa Press rev. date: 09/19/2022

BALBOA.PRESS

15 MINUTES

Written by
Dawna Jean Smith

Illustrated by
Moran Reudor

If you could give her fifteen minutes of your day......

2

You could read
an adventure
about outer space
or meet her for tea
at her little place.

You could learn a funny joke
or sing a funny song

6

Let her stand on your feet
as you dance along.

You could learn about
flowers and bugs and things.
There's plenty in the garden
Even things with wings!

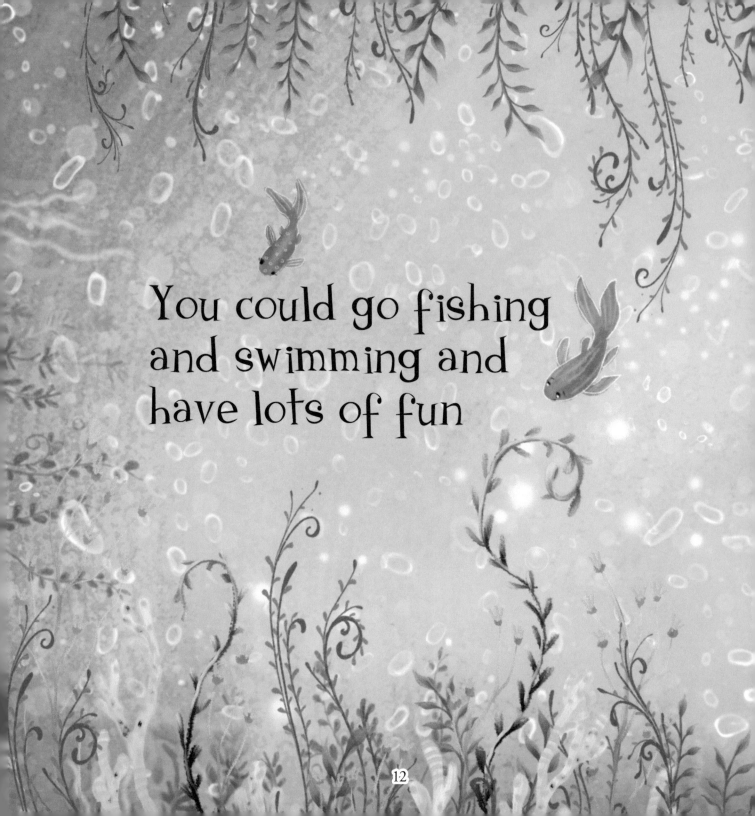

You could go fishing
and swimming and
have lots of fun

12

and you could sit together
and watch the setting sun...

14

When your everyday busy
schedule takes you away,
give her fifteen minutes to
make her day....

special.

The End

Printed in the United States
by Baker & Taylor Publisher Services